shades
of
lovers

catarine hancock

central
avenue
publishing

2020

This is a work of fiction. Names, characters, places and incidents either are the
product of the author's imagination or are used fictitiously and any resemblance to
actual persons, living or dead, business establishments, events or locales is entirely
coincidental.

Published by Central Avenue Publishing, an imprint of Central Avenue Marketing Ltd.
www.centralavenuepublishing.com

SHADES OF LOVERS

Trade Paperback: 978-1-77168-222-0
Epub: 978-1-77168-223-7
Mobi: 978-1-77168-224-4

Published in Canada
Printed in United States of America

1. POETRY / Love   2. POETRY / Women Authors

10 9 8 7 6 5 4 3 2 1

this is a book of poems
about all kinds
of love:

from the sweeping highs
of first love
to the suffocating lows
of toxicity and abuse,

from being completely shattered
to rebuilding myself,

from being left
to being the one who leaves,

from loving others
to the most important thing of all:

loving myself.

love comes in many colors

ruby red — 1

> for two young hearts
> falling in love for the first time,
> only to have one rip the other
> apart at the seams.

ocean blue — 49

> for the love that was not ready
> and bloomed too soon
> between a sad boy and broken girl
> who had no idea how to fix what couldn't be.

primrose pink — 91

> for the sweetness shared
> between these two;
> they had a love like a flower:
> it grew, and blossomed, and wilted.

stormy gray — 119

> for the hurricane that tore
> through her heart and soul;
> she was a boat lost at sea
> and he was determined to sink her.

golden yellow — 181

> for the calm after the storm,
> the sun breaking through the clouds—
> a love meant to save,
> but never meant to stay.

emerald green — 213

> for the planting of a sapling
> of a love that was going to
> take root and grow,
> and last and last and last.

1

ruby red

for two young hearts
falling in love for the first time,
only to have one rip the other
apart at the seams.

did you love me? i'd hope.

did i love you? of course.

did you break my heart? oh, every bit of it.

—some questions and some answers

first love hits at any time.
it doesn't matter if you're 12
or 17
or 25;
first love will take you
whenever it pleases.

it slammed into me at 13
in the form of a lanky boy
with lopsided dimples
and hazelnut eyes,
and it stood back and watched
as he cut me open
and let the words out
for the very first time.

people discredit my writing because i am so young. they always have. i started sharing my heart when i was 13, after you left. writing was all i had to cope, to heal. i am 20 now but people still don't think my words ring true. age to them is an indicator of learning, of wisdom, of weathering.

but listen to me: there are children who are only 10 who have experienced more pain than adults who have lived half a century. there are teenagers who have had more obstacles laid across their paths than my grandparents.

i was not one of those children, nor was i one of those teenagers. my problems are small in the face of theirs. and i am thankful for that.

but that does not mean my pain and my struggles aren't valid.

that does not mean they don't deserve a place on the shelf.

— *a small disclaimer*

first love is unlike anything else.

i still remember how the nerves felt,
how the butterflies flapped around
in my stomach.

the ones you love after
your first will never
feel as exotic or new.

first love is an exploration.

i saw the entire world
in your eyes.

i can't tell you
how many times
somebody has looked
at my open wounds
and told me
that i'm not really
bleeding

— age doesn't mean shit

i wrote my first poem about you, but it wasn't sad. no, this was before. before we came to a screeching halt, before you wrapped your hand around my jugular, yanked, and watched the blood drip down your wrist.

i wish i could find it, but i lost those pages long ago. i remember that i said it didn't matter how long we lasted, that i was just glad to be able to call you mine for at least a while.

how silly of me to think it wouldn't hurt when you left. how foolish of me to not foresee a devastating end.

scene:

we are walking down your street. i catch you staring.
"what are you staring at?" i ask.
"just you," you respond.
"wha—why?"
"because," is all you say.
"why?" i ask again. nervous, for some reason.
"because!"
"why, though?"
"because, you're fucking beautiful!"

end scene

i remember this distinctly. more than our first kiss or the first time you said you loved me.

i remember it because years later, it is horrifying to me.

because later that night, when i went to talk to self-love, i saw you looking back at me when i should have seen myself.

relationship status: it's complicated.

i'm not seeing what i should be seeing when i think of you.

there's somebody else here.

and there shouldn't be, but it feels so good.

is this wrong? is this wrong to be thinking about somebody else when i should be thinking of you (myself)?

i only feel beautiful when they tell me so.

tell me, is that really a crime?

the first boy
i fell in love with
was a writer.

he wrote me love letters,
won me over with metaphors
and mind paint.

i was young
and more in love
with the idea of love
than anything,
but he was the first one
to light a fire in me.

he was also the first one
to put it out.

the first time we kissed
was on saint patrick's day;
i wanted to think that made
us lucky.

—i was wrong

she was the one you liked
first.

but she was unattainable,
so you picked me.

and i knew this,
but i loved you,
so i buried it in the back of my mind
and didn't think about the fact
that i may have been a second choice.

i didn't think about it
until all of a sudden
she was attainable,
and despite having me,
you picked her.

you fucking picked
her.

—i guess i should've seen it coming

you said *i want you to stick this out* like this was a blip in the system and not you confessing your love for another girl,

like this wasn't one of the worst possible things you could do to somebody,

like this was simple, like it was fucking easy, like it was as solvable as algebra,

like saying *i think i'm falling in love with her* to your damn girlfriend was something you could just take back.

but you didn't take it back, you said *i want you to stick this out,* you said *i want you to stay,* you said *please don't go yet,*

and somewhere deep inside of me, the woman i am now stood up and told me to say *no.*

no i will not stay,

no i will not wait around with bated breath while you figure out which one of us you like more,

no i will not stick this out, because you saw this coming and did nothing to stop it.

i'm leaving.
i'm fucking leaving.
it's going to tear me apart
but dammit,
i'm leaving.

that first night, i tried so hard to be positive, changed my instagram bio to "single pringle!"; laughed with my mom about the things you did that annoyed me; talked to my best friends and told them i was fine, that i knew all good things couldn't last, that it was okay, we were going to different high schools anyway, it was gonna go down at some point; pushed the pain down as far as it could go, but eventually, it broke through anyway, because she was texting me, telling me how upset she was about it, how she never wanted this to happen—*i just wanted to be his friend*—because i was slowly putting it all together—*he liked her first he fucking liked her first*—because you were texting me, apologizing and apologizing and begging for another chance—

and it was like, all the laughter and the jokes didn't matter.

at the end of the day, everything was still broken.

the problem with
being in love
when you're 13
is that you have no clue
how to love somebody
without placing your entire
self-worth on them.

if they love you,
you love you.

if they leave,
your self-esteem
goes with them.

— i learned the hard way

you gave me
sonnets and soliloquies:
an entire ocean of words.

when you left,
you did not take them
with you.

tell me,
what else was i supposed to do?

—the beginning

poetry became my crutch.

with tears all wet and silver on my cheeks, i would devour poetry like it was a fuel source. the words would run over my tongue like heartbreak's own chicken noodle soup.

i still can't tell if i started writing so much because i needed to have somewhere to place everything, or if i only did it to have a part of you to hold on to.

that's the strangest thing about first loves: no matter how much you make something your own, there are parts of it that will always have their fingerprint.

i'm not sure if i should blame you
for the parts of the breaking
that you could not control:

like how i kissed three boys
i didn't give a single shit about
because i had let myself be defined
by who i had or didn't have at my side,
and then left them spinning because
they didn't feel like you
(but then again, no one did/could/would),

or how i kept talking to her
because she would give me updates
on how you were doing and i just wanted to
hear that maybe you fucking missed me,
even just a little, and i never did
but i kept on hoping that one day
you might admit it,

or how i started to hate how i looked
in the mirror, and it was hard to eat
but i didn't work to fix that
as hard as i should have. but these were
things that happened after, not during,
and i could have stopped, couldn't i?

yes, i could have, and i know part of me
wanted to, but when you're starving for the feeling
that has been so brutally sucked out of your body
you become desperate to find a new source.
but it wasn't coming from anybody, not them, not you,
certainly not myself, and how dare you make me into this,

how dare you just walk away with barely a speck of rubble

on your clothes, how dare you make me feel ashamed of my
own skin, how dare you leave me, how dare you break me, how
dare—

i can't blame you for this part.
i know i can't; it isn't the right
thing to do.

but they say to trace a problem
back to its source.

and so i follow the red string back to the point
on the map, and it's your face. so what does it mean?

maybe it means you loved me too little.
maybe it means i just loved you too much.

—the breaking

i keep wishing
and wishing
and wishing,
but i am the only
one of us stuck on 11:11.

time has moved on.

— and so have you

you were my first.

first love,
first kiss,
first hand to hold,
first love letter,
first "i love you."

and i spent a long time
trying not to forget that,
since you were also
the first person to
completely
fucking
destroy me.

— i couldn't tell which one was more important

does nostalgia
sink its teeth into you
like it does to me?

do you ever think of the girl
you loved before anyone?

do you ever think of how
you loved her?

how you left her?
how you broke her?

i hate.

i look in the mirror
and pinch the skin
on my stomach and my thighs.

she is prettier than me,
i think,
and she has curvier hips
and is both big and small
in all the right places.

i do not think
i am any
of those things.

so i hate.

not her,
because it wasn't her fault.

but it wasn't my fault either,
and yet,

here i am.

—the dark times

i cry.

i cry in the shower
and in my bed
and sometimes just randomly.

she is stronger than me,
i think,
and she knows more
about everything
and has so much to say.

i do not think
i am any
of those things.

so i cry.

not about her,
because she does not want my tears.

but you don't want them either,
and yet,

here i am.

—the dark times ii

i love.

i love you every second
of every day
of every week you're gone.

she is not permanent like me,
i think,
and she will not stick around.
you will realize she isn't meant
for you and you will come back.

i think
i am all
of those things.

so i love.

not myself,
because i haven't figured out how to.

but you haven't figured out how to love me either,
and yet,

here i am.

—the dark times iii

the months in between were bleak.

i let a boy fall in love with me that i was never going to love back, because i missed the feeling of being wanted—

i did not know how to want myself.

i spent a lot of time reading poetry that begged for a boy to come to the rescue—

i did not know how dangerous that was,

and eventually i let you in again when you came crawling back—

i did not know how to let you go.

things that remind me of you #1

cigarette smoke / bleach cleaner / love letters / shark teeth /
turtle necklaces / the beach / old dogs / lakes / confessionals /
four-leaf clovers / sweaty palms / rushed kisses / tears /

/ tears /
/ tears /

/ sad poems /
/ confused poems /

/ continuous pain /
/ holding on to something that is probably dead /
/ holding on to something that is definitely dead /

/ not letting go /

/ not saying goodbye /

/ not saying goodbye even though i should /

there was a boy right after you, with mahogany hair and ocean eyes, and i let him fall in love with me. he looked at me as if i were the sun, and i, desperate for the warmth of love's light, let him fall in love with me.

i knew there was never a chance. but i took things from him anyway, greedy and hungry. a kiss. a hand. a touch. when i told him i couldn't do it, when i set his heart back in his hands, i wanted to think it was because you had broken me.

you made me incapable of loving somebody.

but it was never that you made me incapable of loving another.

it was that for the longest time, you made me incapable of loving anybody but you.

relationship status: single (and very lonely).

you're not who i want anymore. i want him.

he's the only one who can make me feel like i'm worth something.

i don't love you anymore. i don't like what i see when i look at you (myself).

so now you're gone, and so is he.

and i am left with nothing.

i miss you i type into the message box, but that feels wrong, and
too sad—
backspace backspace backspace

i hate you i type instead, but somehow that feels even less
right—
backspace backspace backspace

i miss you but i hate you—
backspace backspace

i hate you but i miss you—
backspace

i hate you because you lied to me
i hate you because you hurt me
i hate you because everything

but that doesn't seem right to me, either,
because i don't hate you—
backspace backspace backspace

i miss you because you made me feel special
i miss you because you were my friend
i miss you because everything

and i almost hit send, but—

i hit backspace because you don't care
i hit backspace because you don't love me
i hit backspace because everything.

everything, always everything. you are as far away as you will
ever be, and i am still staring at a phone screen.

—the imessage debate

our mutual friend asks if you can talk to me.

why would he want that?
i ask him,
determined to stay strong
and say no.

he wants to apologize.

well, he already did,
and that didn't change anything.

catarine,
he found your poems.

fuck,
i say,
here's my new number.

sometimes, love is fickle.

sometimes, love does not know whether it should

stay

    or go.

it likes for you to leave the door unlocked.
it likes it when you let it keep the key.

so when love comes back with bags filled with

i'm sorry

                    everything is wrong without you

          i read the poems and i want to fix things

please let me fix things,

it can still wedge its foot in the door and kick it open.

love will dump those bags in your hands and say,

look what i brought for you
                can i stay?

and maybe one day,
you will say no.

this time, though,
you say,

of course. i just finished dinner.

you came back.

i spent hours smiling myself silly,
filled with sweetness that made my teeth rot,

because you

came back.

and just like that,
i forgot all the pain
you caused me.

it was like a
light switch.

—the poems said you would save me

maybe you came back
because

you loved me

or

maybe you came back
because

she didn't love you

and

maybe i should have stopped
to ask that question
before i let you
back in
again.

— in retrospect

scene:

we are at your house. it is at the beginning of you fixing things. we are sitting on your couch.

your dad's friend comes by.

"who's this?" she asks.

you look at me and smile.

"this is the girl i love," you declare to her, and place your hand on mine.

you look at me like you want me desperately to believe you. not because you're lying, but because you just want to fix things.

later, you tell me those three words again and again and again. until i believe you.

until i have no choice.

end scene

for a few months, everything is fine.

i don't read as many poems,
and i write even fewer.

i push all the letters
i never got to arrange
back down my throat.
they feel wet and cold
on my tongue but i swallow
them down,
down,
down.

i am convinced
that i do not need
that part of myself
anymore,
and you do not
tell me otherwise.

i think you might be scared
of what will happen
if you do.

so is it love?

when you have to lock away
the most honest part of yourself,

is it love?

i almost thought we got it right,

that we were in the clear,
that maybe,
you had fixed things
like you said
you would.

but then,

she came back.

and just like that,
you forgot
me.

it was like a
light switch.

—the poems fucking lied

i saw it coming
before you did.

so i pushed you
out.
closed my doors
and armed my walls
with catapults.

when you said you wanted
to talk to her,
to be her friend again,

i said,
it's her or me.

teetered on the top
of my castle.
held the chain to the
drawbridge in my hand.

i said,
this should be easy.

you said,
it's not.

i left the drawbridge up.

—you didn't deserve to be let back in

don't give
your love
to someone
who is so
clearly unwilling
to return it

—the pain isn't worth it

i allowed myself to cry for one night, and one night only. i did not mourn you like i did the first time. there wasn't enough energy in me to go through that again. loving you had taken everything out of me. i was drained, sucked completely dry. i did not want to give you any recognition at all. i don't think i ever wrote a poem about what happened the second time until this book. i buried it alive, swallowed it completely whole, stuffed it away on a shelf to become dusty and forgotten.

that night, i swore off second chances. i was convinced that nobody can change, even the people who want to the most. i had spent the first half of my freshman year of high school crying over you and then spent the second half loving you, only to end it crying, again. the same reason. the same girl. the same weaknesses: your romanticism, your sharp mouth, your refusal to see your mistakes. people can change the way they dress and the way they smile, i told myself, but at their core, nobody can change. some people will be doomed to give too much love to those who do not deserve it. i already knew, then, that i was one of those fools.

it hurt less. the pain faded within days. after a few weeks, i don't think i loved you at all. my heart had learned its lesson and my mind was busy gloating. it taunted me for months. i wanted to ask it why it didn't speak up sooner. my mind did not admit that it was in love with you too. years later, it came back and did the same after i let somebody else take chance after chance after chance from me.

i did not answer your texts for days. i wanted you to figure it out on your own. i didn't want to have to spell it out for you. in the end, you stopped texting. you put everything in the right order. she texted me, *why can't you let us be friends?* i told her, *because that's what happened the last time.* i think she started to hate me then. i never told her i knew she loved you. i had always known. i told her, *you can have him.* she blocked my number. i don't know if she ever had you, but she moved away a few months later.

i found the poems in me again. i pulled them out of joints and stomach lining. i spit them out onto the page. i whispered them sweet apologies. i said, *i am sorry i gave you the light and then took it away. i am sorry i promised greatness and then traded you for somebody else.*

i said, *i am sorry for being like him.*

the poems forgave me.

i said, *you really are a part of me,* and then i began to rebuild.

—*on second chances and when to give them*

word of advice #1:

love isn't allowing somebody
to love yourself on your behalf

you are the only one who knows
how to do that

people will come and go

but you
you are
forever

something to know:

your first heartbreak will not
kill you

i promise you it won't
no matter how hard
it becomes to breathe
no matter how terrible
food tastes in your mouth

this is not the end of you

your life does not lie
in the hands of the person
who forgot your worth

it lies in yours

to those of you healing a broken heart for the very first time:

1. the world is not ending. it will keep spinning. you will keep breathing. the flowers will continue to bloom. you will bloom, too.

2. it is okay to be angry. it is okay to want to scream your throat raw. scream at them, if they deserve it. but do not ever try to hurt them as they hurt you. revenge is never what you need. it will not heal you; it will infect you.

3. sometimes, love just dies. there isn't always another lover or an obstacle too large to overcome. sometimes, it just dies. and it doesn't make it any less sad, but it will, in hindsight, make a lot more sense.

4. when you miss them, let yourself, but give yourself a lifeline. something to keep you from falling back into them. delete their number. block them everywhere. miss the love you had, but remember it is no longer here. do not try to find it. you will just find a grave.

5. the world is not ending. it will keep spinning. everything will keep growing, and you? you will keep breathing, and you will be, one day, just fine.

thank you
for the pain
and the poetry

especially
the poetry

— i don't know what i would've done without it

you gave me
the power
to use my words.

and for that,
a part of me
will always
love you.

to ruby red,

even though the poems might sound angry, i promise that i'm not. i laid it to rest a long time ago. writing about you now is like having watched a sad movie a dozen times; eventually, it's just numb. going through the motions. but i tell our story for the many people who need to hear it. there are many lessons to be learned from it.

i know a part of me will always sting when i think about you. i haven't seen you in years, and i honestly don't plan to, ever again. i think that even now, it would be like ripping open an old wound. i know that you are well. i know that you are happy. that is all that matters to me. i have no reason to reach out to you anymore.

i don't want to say you ruined me, because you didn't. you knocked me off balance and maybe to the ground, but you didn't destroy me like i once thought you did. the one who did that was still years away.

i don't know if i will ever forgive you for picking her over me not once, but twice, when it was so obvious that she wasn't going to be there for you like i was. i will always be a little angry and a little hurt. being a second choice when you know you deserved to be the first doesn't stop hurting no matter how long ago it happened. so i know these poems may still seem raw and if you ever read them, they might just hurt your feelings, but know that hurting you was never my intention. it might just be better if you never read them at all.

thank you for igniting in me the fire that has not dimmed since you first broke my heart. thank you for helping me realize that i was more than a sad girl. i know you wanted me to reach for the stars and take what it was that i desired.

i hope you know that i am.

2

ocean blue

for the love that was not ready
and bloomed too soon
between a sad boy and broken girl
who had no idea how to fix what couldn't be.

you were a love of learning.

before you,
i was filled with misconceptions about love
and what it could be.

i did not think love could just be easy—
and with you it could have been.

if only i had listened.

if only i had let it.

—this one was my fault

before anything,
you were my friend.

it didn't take long
for us to find our rhythm.

i spent hours talking
to you.

but while the words
came easily,
my heart did not.

still broken,
still bruised,
i thrust it towards you
when it did not want to go.

stop,
it cried,
i am not ready.
i am still hurting from
the last one.

i should've listened.
i should've listened.
i should've listened.

—but i didn't

perhaps if i had let
us simmer a bit longer,
we would've gone down
the way we should have.

— i drank us cold

question:

how do you make a relationship work
when one half holds the weight of depression
and the other half is too selfish
to help them carry it?

answer:

you don't.

for the first few months of our friendship,
i didn't know.

i didn't know that behind your laugh, your loud voice, your
sense of humor,
there lurked a sadness.

i think i was mad at you for not telling me sooner, but i can't
remember.
there was a lot of anger with us, and i can't place a lot of it in
order.

either way, i never told you,
because i never told you a lot of things.

i never told you how scared it made me,
that i didn't know how to help you.
i never told you how much i missed you, either,
but that wasn't because of the "never" part of us,
it was because of the "too late."

if i told you something it was too late.
i said sorry too late.
i asked if we were okay too late.

in hindsight, i think i told you i loved you too late, too.

don't date somebody
for the purposes of having
an interesting love story,
or a mountain to climb,
or somebody to save.

people aren't
fucking trophies
and their trauma
isn't an award for you
to put on your wall.

so, take a second
and think to yourself:

are you dating somebody
because you love them?

or are you dating them
because you want
everybody else
to love you?

it wasn't that i didn't love you,
it was that i pushed myself into it
when i should have let it sit.

i felt it coming
and i jumped before checking
to see what was waiting below.

i didn't realize i wasn't
ready for impact
until i was already falling.

i didn't know a lot about mental illness, before you.
all i knew about it came from shitty tumblr poems that said
shitty things like

kiss my scars and call me beautiful

vodka reminds me of you

galaxies in my veins

so i sort of thought i could save you, or something fucked up
like that. i thought that heartbreak felt the same as clinical
depression. i thought it was just a pit in your stomach and not
wanting to get out of bed. there was a fucked-up part of me that
thought your sadness was a delicacy, sweet and soft. i thought
of all the ways we could fix each other—how romantic would
that be? what a stunning love story.

but it wasn't like that. at all. i couldn't just kiss you on your bad
days and you would suddenly smile and all the dark clouds
would part to reveal the sun. an "i love you" didn't stop you
from wanting to kill yourself. it went so much deeper than that,
and i was so foolish, so immature. so unready for someone like
you.

i always think about what could have happened if i had known
more. if we had talked more. if you'd helped me understand.

but how could you have explained how it worked when you
barely understood it yourself?

relationship status: it's getting better.

we're on our way. i look at you (me) in the mirror and i don't hate what i see.

i don't love you, but i like you. most of you at least.

i need you more than him, i know that. i know you deserve more love.

and yet.
and yet.

i just can't give it to you.

i did not know
how to love myself
and love you
at the same time

i could either give it all
to you
or all
to me

if i split it down
the middle
we were both left
with too little

and i have never
been one
to disappoint

—the most selfless thing i did for you

this is something
honest:

i felt bad
at loving you.

this is something
terrible:

but i did nothing
to fix it.

this is something
pathetic:

and i still blamed
you when you left.

being bad
at loving someone
doesn't make you a bad person

it just makes you
bad for them

— a thing i didn't understand

word of advice #2:

stop expecting
every love story
to be a perfect fairy tale

sometimes love is messy
sometimes love is sad

and sometimes
so are people

stop running from people
who are harder to understand
because you don't want
to take the time
to figure out
how to love them right

what you said:

i don't think i can trust you
i don't feel comfortable talking to you
about my depression and i should

that's an important part of me
and i should be able to talk to you

but i don't think you want to hear it

what i said:

i know i don't always understand
and i know i don't always know
what to say

but i want to be there for you

i just need to wrap my head around it

you shook your head, then:

you see that's the problem
you still think it's some cute
romance story

you're not going to save me
that isn't how this works

you're too wrapped up in yourself
and how it affects you

always about you
isn't it

then i was crying, and:

i'm trying
i swear i'm trying

and then came the final blow:

no
you aren't

— and that was how we ended

everybody told me that you hated me.

"he thinks you're a bitch,"
they said,
"he hates you."

and deep down,
i think i always knew
that they were feeding me
poison,
but i drank it anyway.

toxins clouded my mind
as i said,
"i hate him too.
he's a piece of shit."

i never heard it from you
but i believed it,

because i thought
it was what
i deserved.

— i had brought this on myself

the biggest crime
was that i was so upset
about our breakup
ruining my image
that i never once
thought about

whether or not
you were okay

if this brought on
a bout of depression

if this made you
want to hurt yourself

maybe
just maybe

for once

i should have
thought about
whether you were
in more pain than me.

— you were right. i was selfish

i told myself, i am not a rehabilitation center.
women do not exist just to fix impossibly broken things.

but you never treated me that way.

i am not a rehabilitation center, this is true.
i am not somebody who exists only to try and fix what i am not able to.

but i was, in that moment, a coward.

i felt your rough edges and blanched at the slightest prick of blood.

and i chalked it up to being immature. i even blamed it on the one before you. i cried that i actually wasn't ready for something new. but i had known that from the beginning, had buried that truth deep in the ground. i dug it from its grave only when i needed something to defend my actions.

but i was a coward.

i was afraid that i wouldn't be able to pull away from my wounds to help tend to yours. i was afraid that you had too many glass shards embedded in your skin to help me pull out the few i had in mine.

so, in the end, i wasn't afraid of you. no.

i was just afraid of myself.

you told me,
"i don't think i ever meant that much
to you in the first place,"

and my heart broke,
because you were wrong,
but i barely had
any evidence to prove it.

for a year
we never spoke.

avoided each other
like the plague.

i wrote
and you drew back
into yourself.

we both tried
to ignore the
gaping hole
we left
in each other's
lives.

—we both lost a best friend

you catch my eye from across the room.

i want to wave. your hand moves like you're going to.

but then we notice that people are watching. your hand stays down. i look at my feet.

when i look back up, you are still looking at me.

for a moment, we just stare. then you offer up a soft, sad smile. just a slight upturning of the corners of your mouth.

i don't need to hear you say it to know that you miss me just as much as i miss you.

end scene

for the first time in months, i type in your phone number. i type out an apology. i don't send it, but i almost do. a moment doesn't mean forgiveness. you still might not want anything to do with me.

when you text me three days later, the first thing i do is smile.

things that remind me of you #2

the color blue / flannels / late nights in front of a laptop under
the blankets / skype calls / bedtime / hidden handholding / the
true meaning of friendship / uncertainty / movie theaters / ben
howard /

/ not understanding /
/ not really trying to /

/ realizing you didn't know anything /
/ realizing just a little too late /

/ not knowing if you just lost a best friend /
/ or if you lost everything else too /

we began to fix things,
slowly but surely,
brick by brick.

we rebuilt this house
of ours,
put wood in the fireplace
and lit it.

and then,
we said everything
we had needed to say
since the beginning.

—it was almost like starting again

i think it will always
feel a little more
my fault than yours—

the destruction
you left in your wake
was nothing compared
to the ruin
left in mine:

a rainstorm
to an F5 tornado.

—i was always worse

i will never
forgive myself
for hurting you
like i did.

it sits on my
throat like a
deadweight.

—guilt

i told you
that i thought we could
have been great together.

you told me
that we still could be.

it was in that moment
that i realized two things:

one: i did not love us
anymore.

and

two: a part of you
still did.

we still could be
still echoes around
in my head.
i mull over the words
on days where i find myself
entrapped in the past's arms.

at the time,
i met those words
with silence.

i knew what
they meant,
what was laced around
each letter.

i knew it was a question,
not a statement.

i said,
i wanted us to work so badly.
i wanted us to be great.

we still could be,
you replied,
the question mark silent
but deafeningly loud at the same time.

you were asking
if i wanted to.

you were asking

if i thought so.

i never gave you an answer.

but here is my answer, now.

darling, i could have loved you more than the trees love the sun, but we couldn't be.

the honest truth is that we were never meant to be great. we were never going to work like that. i was always going to be too blind and you were always going to be too fucking stubborn, and i was always going to try to save you even after i figured out that i couldn't, and you were always going to resent me for it.

another chance for us meant this. it meant figuring out how to push things back together. it meant saying sorry and laughing a few times about ignorance and mistakes and then leaving it.

and maybe another chance means leaving things feeling open. unbuttoned. unscrewed.

there isn't anything here for us, don't you see that? there isn't anything left. we're a skeleton.

i can still miss the way you'd make me laugh with just one word. i can still long for those never-ending phone calls.

i can still want to find somebody who can fill your shoes.

i can, and i do. every day.

but when you said
we still could be,

that didn't stop my heart from saying,
no.
we couldn't.

— my answer

the words *i'm sorry* became my best friends.

they rolled off my tongue every second as we sat there unearthing every crack in the foundation, every broken windowpane. and they became yours, too, because we found breakage in places i never touched: cracked china, ripped curtains.

we had built a home on lies and insincerity, on fairy-tale tropes and misinformation. your secrets were nailed into the beams. my selfishness was trapped in the drywall. everywhere, the air was heavy. thick with all that was wrong.

so, we tore away the rot and the brokenness. tossed out the garbage. at night, we sat around the fire and apologized, over and over again. until we knew only of forgiveness and learning.

this isn't another love story. this is a reconciliation.
this was never going to end with us together.

in the end, we left the house and never looked back. you turned one way and i turned another.

the house we built, it is stronger now. i want to think it can withstand the weather and time in our absence. i want to think that there may be a time where we come back.

— *renovation*

i think
we may always
be a little drawn
to each other

because what else
can you do
when your love story
was never finished?

when there are pages
still not read

how do you just
put it down?

—we will always be unfinished

love is not always perfect,
no matter how desperately
you want it to be.

it always has
a point to prove.

i could not understand
the lesson love was trying
to teach me.

i could not love you
the way you needed me to,
because i still did not know
how to love myself.

you were such a long beginning with such a fast, quick end. it was like a door being locked tight just as we reached for the handle.

sometimes i think about what might have been waiting on the other side.

— i doubt i'll ever know

a few weeks ago
i saw that you were
with a girl
and that she made you
the happiest you've ever been.

thank god,
i remember saying to myself,
thank god you are finally
getting the love that
you deserve.

i know
we don't speak
often,

but i'm still here
if you need me.

on the off chance
you find yourself
alone again,

i will be here.

always.

—that's what friends are for

i am a girl
who has been broken
but that
is not
the reason
i am beautiful

— i will always be more than my pain

love
should not feel
like you're constantly
doing somebody a favor.

love
should not feel
like a waste of
your time.

if you look at them
and can already feel
them draining you,

go.

it is not your time.

they are not your person.

i do not exist
just to satisfy
your savior complex

—take your white-knight bullshit somewhere else

you once said
that you did not like to read
my poetry because
it upset you.

i hope that if you ever
read this,
you will find yourself
smiling with the knowledge
that i have grown into
the kind of person
who is less selfish
and more thoughtful,
less angry
and more gentle,
less sad
and wiser.

i hope that
you will smile,
knowing that i have
taken what you taught me
and taught it to
everyone who would listen.

to ocean blue,

it's been too long since we last spoke. i have to say, even now, i find myself missing your friendship. i hope that one day we find time to sit down and really try to make something grow again. i would like that. i think the wounds are healed.

you were, when we were close, always the better half. even though i didn't know that at the time (or i did know, i just didn't want to admit it), you were a lot kinder than i was. i think that, despite all the growing i've done, you still might be. and perhaps that is due to what you've gone through—the things you told me that i would never dare write in this book. no, you trusted those with me, and i would not dare betray that trust.

i didn't want you to be a lesson. and although i am grateful for what you taught me about the mind and heart, i do wish i had been ready to just love you. i think our high-school years would have been a lot more peaceful.

i believe that you are well on your way to happiness, if you haven't already reached it, and for that, i am endlessly thankful. there is nothing more that i could ever want for you. you deserve it a thousand times over.

i miss you, still. not sadly, but happily. with a smile on my face. much like the smile you always brought about when you were here.

3

primrose pink

for the sweetness shared
between these two;
they had a love like a flower:
it grew, and blossomed, and wilted.

if you had let me
i would have given you
my entire heart

all the love
in my tired body

it would have been yours
even if you never asked
because that is just
what i did

that is what i understood
love to be

but you pushed it back to me
when i held it out for you

keep it
you said
you need some of this love
for yourself

it was the strangest thing:
realizing that loving somebody
did not mean giving them
the means to
destroy you

you were the gentlest love i ever touched. a whispering pink. it was soft on my skin. melted on my fingers like cotton candy.

you were the first boy i straddled while kissing. you stripped away the parts of my innocence i didn't need to keep, and i was glad it was you who did it, because i was taking parts of yours too. step by step, we moved together, though never side by side.

i think we both knew deep down we were doomed from the start. you can say you wanted to marry me but you didn't. i wasn't made for you and you knew it as well as i did. i think you're someone who doesn't like to admit that they might be wasting their time. you fell in love with me so you thought, surely this must be it. why else would i bother.

but to me, you were not a waste of time. you were a milestone. a climax. you were the moment of realization. that love is not all-taking. that love does not have to consume you to be real. you can love and sleep soundly. you can love and kiss softly. you can love and leave quietly.

you can love and leave whole.

relationship status: on the outs

i guess one could say we aren't on speaking terms. i try my hardest to avoid you, but sometimes i can't help but catch your eye (in the mirror). and there are moments where you still take my breath away. there are times where i almost love you again.

he wants me to come back to you. he says he won't have me otherwise.

maybe he's right.

maybe it is time to finally fix things with you (me).

i never saw you
in my future

and it didn't bother me
one bit.

i was happy
and so were you
and for once
i was not so wrapped
up in what was coming
that i couldn't enjoy
what was already there.

the only memories
i have of you
are kind

you
playing with my younger brother

you
helping my mom carry in the groceries
without her even asking

you
driving my friends home when they didn't
have rides

you
hugging me when i told you
about my first heartbreak

you
opening the car door
on our first date

you
loving me even when i couldn't figure out
how to love you back

i only remember
the sweetness of you

a sweetness that i always knew
did not belong
with me

word of advice #3:

when a love comes along
that helps you love yourself

hold it
as close
as you can

when a love treats you
like you're supposed to be treated

cherish it
as long
as you can

and when that love can leave
without breaking your heart

let it
as gently
as you can

you were easy to love.

sweet like sugar,
you melted over my tongue
like candy.

there was never a bitter
aftertaste left in my mouth,
not even at the end.

—raspberry flavor

i read somewhere that if a rose gets its thorns cut off it will die faster.

that was us, i think:
all soft and silky.

a rose without its thorns.

no prick. not even a drop of blood
was spilled at our hands.

— in other words, it was too good to be true

scene:

we are walking up and down my street. it's about six months before we start dating. i am just getting to know you. you are telling me about how the girl you like isn't being nice to you. i tell you, then, about the boys before you, how they broke me and i broke them.

you hug me. "i'm sorry," you say, "you don't deserve that pain."

"i know that," i respond, "i just don't know how to stop it from happening."

"someone will show you what a good love is like one day. one day, you'll know what it's like to have somebody who is just good."

end scene

did you hope, even then, that it would be you?

i cannot tell
if i took you for granted

or if i just didn't understand
how special it was
to find a love
that was purely selfless
and completely kind

— i learned soon enough

you were the one
i did not see coming

perhaps
that is why
it was okay
when you couldn't
stay

you kissed me like we had all the time in the world,
and that's when i knew i was not meant for you.

i wanted hungry.
i wanted someone who knew everything was a ticking time
bomb, who knew every kiss could be our last.

i wanted someone who was so afraid to lose me,
every touch carried a bag to tuck a memory in.

we didn't have all the time in the world.
you knew this and turned the other way.

i wanted somebody who faced it head on.
loved me harder just to spite it.

we were always too different to be able to last,
and i don't say that like it's a bad thing,
i say it like that's okay, like that's normal,
because it is.

i fell in love with you because you showed me
a kindness in love that i had not seen yet,
a kindness that i would not see after you for a long time,
a kindness i did not appreciate as much as i should have.

i found the simplicity of us intriguing first,
irritating second, and destructive last.

we were always running out of time.

nothing about us ever really clicked into place. in a weird, disjunct type of way, we moved as one.

everybody could tell something about us was always slightly out of sync.

everybody except us, it seemed.

you see,
i was just so tired
of being the one
who was left.

i was so tired
of having attachments
chopped in half
without any warning,
of having my heart dropped
and shattered on the ground
without giving me any time
to try and catch it.

so the one time we fought,
i saw the end hidden behind
every single word.
every *you're too much of this*
and *you're not enough of that*
screamed another message,
loud and clear:

i am falling out of love with you.
i am going to leave you.
this is the end.
this is the end.
this is the end.

i don't even know if you knew it yet,
but i did.

and i was just so tired
of being the one
who was left.

things that remind me of you #3

actual dates / meeting my grandparents / forrest gump / ease /
peace and quiet / laundry detergent / cautious touches / gentle
questions / silver pendants / flashlight tag / going to church
for the first time / separating loving another person and loving
yourself /

/ knowing my worth /
/ knowing my beauty /
/ knowing it for the first time /

/ learning love can just be easy /
/ learning that doesn't mean that it's forever /
/ learning that walking away doesn't always have to hurt /

/ feeling love die /
/ feeling love die and being okay with it /

it was followed by a silence
i could only describe as dying:

the final ember's glow faded.
the butterflies laid their wings
down for the very last time.

— our last kiss

before you,
i didn't know
love could
end like that.

soft and quiet,
like falling asleep.

it was after
we ended
that i realized:

you were the first one
to make me feel beautiful
that didn't take it with you
when you left

— i knew better than to let you

you were my rose, my glowing flower. i did everything to keep you alive and well.

but the storm came and it rained. i thought it would stop, but it kept raining, and raining, and raining. and your petals drooped under the weight, and your stem broke, and the storm kept on, flooding me with its rain until i could see nothing else. and eventually i let it. embraced the feeling of it against my skin and forgot how it felt to love a rose like you.

i am so sorry.

if only i had known
what was coming next

maybe i would not
have been
so quick
to run

—hindsight

i find solace
in knowing
that by letting you go
i let you fall right into
the arms of
your soulmate

—you were destined for her

i find solace
in knowing
that by letting you go
i eventually fell into
the arms
of mine

— and i was destined for him

the morning after

i woke up

smiled in the mirror
hugged myself

said
i am beautiful

and believed it.

i think
you would
be proud.

to primrose pink,

when i think about you, i always smile. you are nothing if not a fond memory. you are perhaps one of the most important loves i've ever had, because you never once hurt me. you were the one who showed me that love did not always have to be destructive. you were the one who showed me how a good relationship works, how a stable relationship works, how a real relationship works. it took me awhile to appreciate that, but i learned my lesson eventually.

i know i was not the easiest person to be with. i was insecure but somehow overconfident at the same time, always moving at warp speed and dragging you behind me. i wanted you to be somebody you couldn't be. i wanted you to match me. and you couldn't. it wasn't in your nature.

where the others were rough and jagged, you were soft and smooth. and i loved that, but it made me worry. i am not so soft, like you. i have hard edges and prickly thorns. i was so afraid of cutting you by accident. i was so afraid of causing you to harden.

we were kind, and we were good. but near the end, i started to feel a little bit trapped. i think that is why i fell straight into the one after you. he was so different. i felt like i could breathe again.

it was you who pulled me back to my feet, and you who let me go into the world, full fury. then you stepped back into her, where you had always belonged.

i think the end felt a little bit like being set free, for both of us.

4

stormy gray

for the hurricane that tore
through her heart and soul;
she was a boat lost at sea
and he was determined to sink her.

have you ever felt a love
so fiery that you were
afraid it would burn you
alive?

—spoiler alert: it did.

if you are reading this,
go ahead and flip through
these next 50 pages.

read these poems.

this is our love's burial ground,
after all.

it's only fitting
you should be invited
to the funeral.

you weren't bad at the start, but no love is.

but i feel like you—and they—should know that i still remember how it felt when it was light, and happy, and kind.

i remember every second before the storm rolled in.

we only had a few moments of sun, anyway.

your touch sent an electric shock straight to my heart.

i should have known.

god, i should've fucking known.

— you were going to hurt

the poems about blood started with you.

dripping arteries, jagged wounds, tattered skin—it all began with you.

i sit down to write about you and all i think is disaster.

i compare you to a gunshot wound. to a shark attack. to being on the front line for a hurricane.

i think that was the quietest way of ruining me.

you took my poetry and made it violent.

after the dust had settled,
you spent a lot of time trying to reassure everybody
that there were good parts about us.

"we loved each other a lot, you know,"
you would say,
as if lots of love cancels out lots of abuse.
it doesn't.

"there were good parts about us,"
you would tell me,
as if i wasn't aware, like i didn't write a poem
with that as the literal first line.

i think you thought that, amongst all the hatred and rage,
i had forgotten why i fell in love with you in the first place.

i don't ever forget that.
that isn't what you have to worry about.

no, what you have to worry about
is what i do with that first flame.

i might cherish those memories with a smile,

or i might rip them apart in my head
until i don't understand what the point of us was

at all.

relationship status: it's complicated (again)

we were okay. happy, even. i could smile at the thought of how you (i) would look. i would even be excited to see you (myself).

but suddenly, you're gone, and he's everywhere.

and i can feel it creeping in once more: the urge to leave. to throw myself into him.

at some point, i stop fighting it.

i'm sorry. again.

how do you light a fire
in someone
yet put it out
at the same time?

it was a constant cycle
of back and forth;

one minute i was burning,
the next i was drowning.

i no longer knew
what was worse:

to be hurt by you,
or to be in love with you
despite it.

scene:

we rarely got to see each other, but when we did, it was more than special.

there were three days where we were together at a convention for school.
three days of sneaking around, three days of touches and looks and words.

i kiss you in the stairwell, and you press me up against the wall.
everything is fire.
when i leave, you hold me.
"i love you," you say, "more than anything."

i walk away believing it.

end scene

ten minutes later, you made out with another girl.

did you ever mean a thing you said to me?

this is an angry poem.
it is bloody and it is wounded and it is angry.

i keep saying that this will be the last thing.
the last metaphor, the last analogy.

i keep telling myself that this will be the last poem,
but you're so fucking easy to write about because it's so fucking
easy for you to get under my skin. you never even left.

and you don't even do anything, that's the funny part.
you don't do a damn thing, because you don't care anymore.
you're gone. disappeared. you do not give a shit about me,
but the songs still do. the poetry still does.

how easy it must have been for you to leave such a permanent
mark on me. i'm as impressionable as clay. slam your hand into
me and walk away laughing because the mark will still be here
months after you've washed your hands of me.

i wake up every morning and i say, "today is the last day."
but my body, still molded by your fingertips, says, "no. not yet."

this is an angry poem.
it is bloody and it is wounded and it is angry.

angry at what?
i'm not even sure anymore.
some days i think i'm still angry at you but really, i think i'm
just angry at myself for not being able to get you out of my skin.

— i just can't get rid of you

despite all the lies
you told me

and the half-truths
that danced past
your lips

despite all the words
tied to me that dragged
me
   d
     o
       w
         n

i was too ~~blind~~
to see that you were
only
    bre a k
         ing

   m e

because that is
    love
in its <u>cruelest</u> form

    —br e ak

you fed me apologies
out of your hand
like i was your fucking dog.

— and i ate them right up

i don't think you know
just how badly
i wanted us
to make it.

— i would have bet my life on it

i want to apologize

to all the would-be lovers
i pushed away without
giving them a chance,

to all the friends
i didn't listen to
because they didn't "understand."

to everyone
who saw this coming
so much earlier
than i did.

sometimes you can be toxic too. sometimes you do something to hurt them just because you feel like they deserve it. sometimes you turn into the person who's poisoned you the most. sometimes you let it happen. sometimes you think it's the only way to live anymore. that it's easier to be cruel. that it's simpler to be fake. that the right way to live is by ensuring other people don't. that breaking hearts is the only way to keep yours safe. but let me tell you something: it is not the only way. you are a victim of circumstance. you begin to become toxic when it is the only thing you know anymore. when it is what holds you at night and kisses you good morning. please fight that poison. i beg you to fight it. it is not the only way to live. the people who are the most toxic, who hurt people and look the other way, who jump from heart to heart and leave nothing but destruction in their path, who think it's all fun and games— they are less alive than anyone. they are the ones not living, who have hearts that beat but don't bleed. do not be fooled by their stone-cold exterior. they may seem better off, but they are dead. on the inside, they are dead.

you broke me quietly.

so quietly,
that i didn't even notice
all the cracks
until you were long

g o n e.

sometimes i worry that maybe i asked for too
much

but all i wanted was
honesty

all i wanted was your truth

i asked if you had kissed her
and getting the answer
was like pulling a
mosquito from tree sap—

sticky and messy
and damn near impossible

i ask you now if you always meant
to lie to me

you say no
of course not

but my fingers still feel
a little bit
stuck

—you just couldn't help yourself

i loved you
so damn much.

almost more than
how much
i hated
the way our love
felt under my skin.

—i could feel it poisoning me

if you ever wondered what / it felt like to have an iron chain /
cuffed / to your carotid / then meet somebody like
/   / like you / i don't know how it feels / to not have
you branded / into my skin /

hey / you know / who you are /
your name is
                                    /   /

you know / what / you did /
you
                                                    /   / me

                                                    /   / me

 / insert what you want here because you did it / me

i'm trying not to love you by forgetting your name / but the
weight of it will always / be / here
                                        like /   deadweight /

                    like /   an anchor /

like /   you /

                                                like /   /

                                                like /   /

what's pathetic / is that these blanks / are filled for me / that no
matter what / i would put your name there / every time

                            /   /

you feel the

shape   of my
heart as it   sits in the
palm of your hand. i tell
you to please, be careful,
and you smile. you say
of course you will,
you would never
do a thing that
would ever
hurt me.
so,
tell me,
wh y
is
m y   hea rt,
w hy   i   s

e   e y
v   r   thin g,

wh y is
it   a l
l
s o
brok
en?

i ask
is this love?

and you kiss me
yes

and you take my heart
and it snaps
and it bleeds
and it cracks
and it breaks
and it breaks
and it breaks

and you leave
and you leave
and you leave

and i stay
and i stay
and i stay—

is this love
is this love
is this love—

well it has to be

if i'm still here
it has to be

doesn't it?

you:

didn't make time for me
lied to me
cheated on me
manipulated me
gaslighted me
ignored me

and when i finally broke free
you still had the audacity
to be angry about it
and make it out to be
all
my
fault.

— are you fucking kidding me?

word of advice #4:

when you think
things are starting
to go south—

and not south in a
"we're having some
minor bumps in the road"
way

but south in an
"i can't trust a single
word that comes out
of their mouth"
way—

take
your shit
and

RUN

at some point
i turned into a fool
who was
always in love
with someone
who was
~~sometimes~~ never
in love
with me

i think in shades of red,
like colors of lipsticks
or hues of roses,
and sometimes
i see people in red, too.

one person is a ruby,
another a deep maroon,

and you were blood,
swimming in it,

it just took me too long
to realize that it was
mine.

there was a time
when you controlled
everything i did

i was held captive
by strings tied
to your fingers

even now
i don't know what's
more terrible:

the fact that
you saw the love i had
for you and
used it against me

or the fact that
i let you

—your little puppet

i remember / your sugarplum lips / kisses wet / like a june
thunderstorm / i remember / how your hands / could leave me
/ static / you were that electric / we fit together / like a jigsaw
puzzle / we fit together / like a key and a lock / like something /
meant to be / something / good / trustworthy / permanent /

i want to know / where the wheels fell off / where the blue of
your eyes / started to look more / like thunder / when did you
become the end of me / i keep asking your picture / when did
you decide it would be more fun / to hurt me / than to love me
/ does my blood taste good / is it nice and red / tell me / are you
enjoying / yourself

—when something starts out being more than good
and ends up being more than bad

"you were so far away,"
you said,
"what was i supposed to do?"

a sob caught in my throat
as i replied, "love me.

"you were just
supposed
to love me."

—it wasn't that fucking complicated

i would have died for you
and you would have let me
if it meant you would have
walked away
just fine

—you would have let me drown

i should have been the only one
i should have been the only on
i should have been the only o
i should have been the only
i should have been the onl
i should have been the on
i should have been the o
i should have been the
i should have been th
i should have been t
i should have been
i should have been e
i should have been en
i should have been eno
i should have been enou
i should have been enoug
i should have been enough
i should have been enough f
i should have been enough fo
i should have been enough for
i should have been enough for y
i should have been enough for yo
i should have been enough for you

—but i wasn't

hey siri: how can you tell if somebody really loves you?

retrieving results for "how to tell if somebody really loves you."

hey siri: what do you do if you think he's lying to you? what do you say to him?

i'm sorry, i'm not sure i know what you mean.

siri, how do you know when time is up on your relationship?

i'm sorry, i'm not sure—

what do i do if he's hurting me?
what do i do if he's manipulating me?
what does gaslighting mean?
how do you know?

retrieving results for "characteristics of abusive relationships"

siri, how do i get out?

siri, how does it end?

siri, when will this stop hurting?

i'm sorry, i don't know how to answer that.

… me neither.

—*hey siri*

the other girls
and me,

we are all just
girls
you broke.

there's a sort of
solidarity in that,
isn't there?

so we aren't
enemies,
like i'm sure
you wanted
us to be.

no,
we're yours.

— and we will make you pay

how could you tell a girl
that i told you
you couldn't leave me
for another

when i didn't even know
another
existed?

—plot holes

things that remind me of you #4

secrets / star gazing / can't take my eyes off of you / long car
rides / faulty internet connections / kik messenger / panic
attacks / not knowing if i'm remembering something even
though the texts are right in front of me / letting you lie / letting
you lie again and again and again / backseats of cars / church
parking lots / loving somebody too much / knowing it's too
much but not taking anything back for myself

/ wondering when it will stop hurting /
/ all this fucking hurting /

/ everything /
/ i just see you /
/ in everything /

i wish i could burn you. every page of my story that you're on. i wish i could set fire to all that we were and watch it crumble to ash. at least then, you wouldn't be around to haunt me. or would you? would the smoke swirl in my lungs and clog my throat? would the flames burn my fingertips and scorch the sleeves of my shirt? i'm not sure i know the answer anymore, because the more and more i try to light a flame to us, the more and more seared into my memory you seem to become.

—branding

i know i promised it in the last book, and the book before that, but:

i'm going to put you down after this.

i swear i'm going to put you down.

— i'm sorry i can't keep this promise

i saw you for the first time in a year this week. and for the whole night after, i was so fucking angry. we spoke, and i was screaming inside. my nails were digging crescent moons into my thighs. i kept thinking, why is he talking to me, i don't want him to talk to me. and i think what left me boiling was that i could tell you knew i didn't want you there. but you kept going, kept smiling and saying, that's so great. i'm so happy for you. and i just fucking smiled right back and told you that it was, and that i was having a great time. but you knew. you knew about the cracks under my skin. you knew about the poems. i wonder if this was your kind of vengeance. i've written so many times about my hatred of you, about how much i wanted to never see you again, that this is your way of getting back at me for putting our story out there for everyone to see. this is what i get, isn't it? a cornered conversation where i have to act like the walls aren't closing in on me, because everyone is watching. the girl with her ex-lover that should have rocked the world. the girl with her abuser that is now making her drown in a crowded room. i wanted to scream at you. i wanted to grab her and tell her everything you'd done to me, and to all the others, but i couldn't. because she has no part in this. maybe you've changed. maybe you treat her the way we should've been treated. i hope so, for her sake. at your core, i think that you'll always be at least a little bit cruel. but she doesn't know this. she just knows that i'm crazy and overdramatic, obsessive over what you probably told her was just a botched relationship and not a toxic pool that left my skin rotting. but it was you, it was you that did it, that left me so fucked up, it is you that still fucks me up. i don't know how to separate being civil and hurting myself. i shouldn't have to feel the walls closing in on me for the sake of being nice. i'm more important than that. i shouldn't be so afraid to walk away from you. i have the right, after everything. i know that i do.

but i didn't, and i won't, because i can't. because sometimes it's easier to feel like i'm drowning because for one second, there's a moment in conversation where we slide back into the way we used to be, and for one second, everything doesn't feel so fucking disconnected and broken. for one second, i don't hate being here in this place with you, because it feels how it used to. i take those seconds and run, and i hate to admit it, but i hold them close, because there are times when i don't think you were really in love with me at all, and i doubt that you ever even gave a shit, but in those few moments, i know that at least part of us was as real as it could have been. part of us wasn't so completely and utterly fucked from the beginning. it's strange to cherish those pieces from somebody who ruined me, i know. but i feel like i'm writing about a ghost sometimes. i feel like i'm writing about someone who was never really there, something that never really happened, because it feels too nasty. i wanted to tell you to leave me alone but i also wanted to tell you that i never wanted this. no part of me ever wanted this. and to thank you for giving me something that reminded me that there was something good in you and in us, because i had long since forgotten how that felt. and then i wanted to look at her and i wanted to tell her to run.

— all in a conversation

why did loving you
have to be
so goddamn messy?

i am still scrubbing
you out of
my skin.

—remaining

i have been working
to redefine love,

to open a dictionary
and rip out the words
that are printed there:

you, you, you.

you see,
when you love somebody
for too long and too much,
they morph definitions
into dungeons,
connotation
into chains.

so i have been working
to redefine love,
to break free of this prison
you've locked me in.

i swear to god,
one day your name
will not be there
in my name's place.

—redefining love

do you know
how hard it is
to see the
person you want
to forget most
in everything you love?

—you haunt me

this pain,
it has stuck with me for three years.

it started the day i met you,
and has not left since.

i don't know how to make this any easier for myself.
i don't know what to do with this ache—
i just know i don't want it anymore.

i told myself i had forgiven you,
but if i have, why does it still burn?

if i've forgiven you,
why are there still so many
poems left in me to write?

if i've really let this go,
why does everything
still hurt so
fucking
much?

—the answer is because i haven't

it's amazing how easy it was
for you to break me.

but it's also amazing
how easy it is
for me to marinate
in all this hurt.

it's like i am determined
to make it good,
to make this pain feel
less like a prison cell
and more like a rose garden—

to transform it into
something beautiful
and pretty for everybody
else to reap the benefits of.

they smell the roses
but they don't cut themselves
on the thorns:
they admire the petals
but don't have to wash
their hands of all the dirt.

the truth is that
it's so much easier
to think that there's
a way this could
be beautiful.

but there isn't.

nothing about *this*—

the crying, the shaking,
the anxiety, the attacks,
the paranoia, the trust issues,
the anger, the confusion,
the hatred, the grief,
the healing, the haunting,
the remembering, the analyzing,
the apologizing, the freezing,
the pain, the pain,
the pain, the pain—

is beautiful.

i wish time
were less cruel.

i wish i had forgotten
what it felt like
to love you
before i knew
what sat behind
your smile:

that fire, that burn,
that heartbeat,
that mouth.

i wish time
would let me forget,
i wish time
knew i'd learned
my lesson.

i wish time
would let it go.

i wish i could
stop seeing your face
every time somebody
sings that godforsaken song,

i wish time
would let me forget
the sound of your voice.

which is to say,
i wish i could just forget.

which is to say,
time would let me forget
if i wanted it badly enough.
which is to say,
maybe i am not ready
to forget you
yet.

you can keep calling
all of us crazy
and overdramatic,

you can write off
my poetry as just me
being an obsessive bitch,

you can say your ex
who warned me to stay away
is just bitter and out to get you,

but maybe it's you.

for once,
could you consider
that it's not us?

that maybe
you don't just
find yourself dating
girls who are

crazy
obsessive
bitches
bitter
vindictive

and maybe
you might
be turning us
into that?

i want to think that there's
a reason i fell in love with you.
i want to think that sometimes
that reason still shows itself.

— i know you're not all bad

it's just that all i see
is the wreckage you leave
behind and i can't help but think,
how could somebody do this by accident?

— i'm just having a hard time believing it

sometimes i think about you
and my heart breaks, again.

even now.
even still.

the hardest thing
i have had to learn
is how to stop placing
my worth into the hands
of people who do not know
how to love me.

— you must learn it too

i won't love anybody
the way i loved you

and i am oddly
at peace with that

some nights, i dream about you.

in my dreams, we do not burn the way we did.
there is no scarring. no blood.
in my dreams, we are given a peaceful end.
in my dreams, we get an ending that i don't need to write about.

in my dreams, you smile at me and i am not scared of what you
will say.
in my dreams, you say you're sorry.
in my dreams, i say, "what for?"
in my dreams, you have no reason to apologize.

some mornings, i wake up with tears in my eyes.
some mornings, i almost miss you.

in my dreams, you love me in a way that doesn't break me.
in my dreams, you love me the way you promised you would.

most mornings, i wake up and ache.
most mornings, i hate you for trespassing.

in my dreams, you beg forgiveness.
in my dreams, i am able to grant it.

in my dreams, you blow away like sand.
i watch you fade like a memory.
in my dreams, i watch you go and nod my head in goodbye.
in my dreams, i am able to let you go.

every morning, i think about what could have been.
every morning, i am glad you are not here.

to you, my meteorite lover.

so you know i haven't forgotten.
so you know i can still smile about you.
so you know that i still understand the point of us.

here, for you, my very own train wreck of a romance.
here are the good parts.

good part #1:

you were the first to make me feel once in a lifetime.
you were the original idea of a soul mate.
you told me, "i'm just really glad i met you,"
and that made me feel important.
that made me feel like i could change a heart other than my
own.
that made me feel as if this was worth something,
you were the first person to really make love feel like it was
worth something.

good part #2:

our love story was otherworldly.
we had all the odds stacked against us,
but we loved each other anyway.

they thought we would make it.
we thought we would make it.

i think about the power we held in our hands
before things turned black, and slimy, and bad.

together, we could have lit the world on fire.

good part #3:

sometimes, i can still write about you
as if there's a chance for us (even though there's not).

all things considered,
that's pretty fucking good.

good part #4:

you loved me.
in some weird, sick way, you loved me.
and it will never make what you did to me okay,
and it even makes it a little more painful,
but i know you loved me.

there was a time when i didn't think you did.

good part #5:

i know that sometimes you miss me,
and i want you to know that sometimes,
i miss you, too.

i can't come back to you,
and i never would.

but sometimes,
i miss the parts of you that didn't hurt
so damn much.

good part #6:

i can write down that i miss you
and not be so afraid of it.

it's okay to miss some things,
even if you don't want them back.

good part #7:

when we talked about our future,
it felt tangible.
it felt like it was a hair's breadth away.

we would sing opera together,
we would love each other on stage
and off.

for the first time, i didn't feel like i had to choose
between what and who i loved.

you were the one who taught me i could have both.

good part #8:

that valentine's day message you sent me?
i kept screenshots of it for months after everything
exploded.

i had to remind myself that we had a point somehow.

good part #9:

i chose to cherish the good parts instead of forgetting that we
had a point.

good part #10:

it was with you that i learned to break away from people
who hurt me more than they do anything else.

it was with you that i grew the most (despite never asking to).

you showed me how love is a being. it has a heart that beats. it
has skin that tears. it bleeds, more than any of us. i treat love a
lot more tenderly now.

i realized that running from the storm isn't cowardly; it's smart.
it's survival. it's necessary. you pushed my head under the waves
and inadvertently taught me how to swim.

good part #11:

i can write this and say all these things
and still never want you back in my life.

this is and isn't a thank-you letter.

thank you for making me learn to save myself.
thank you for showing me that a powerful love doesn't always
equal a good love.

i am not thanking you for all the shit you did to hurt me.
i am not thanking you for lying and gaslighting and guilt-
tripping me.

this is acceptance.
this is growth.
this is the final stitch in a wound that has been open for far too
long.

—the good parts

i will not let you be the last one to make me write poems.
i will   last.
      let   me write
   not   on
        you.
i will not let you   make me write.
        you
will not   be the   one to
           last.
   not   you.
   not   you.
   not   you.
i   write poems.
   not   you.
   not   you.
   not   you.

          s o

        th   i   s.

i   s

       the last   poem.

to stormy gray,

i have written book after book, poem after poem, line after line about you. to try and make this feel a little bit better, to try and understand what happened to us.

and this is the last time.

i am putting us down. i have to.

writing about you is no longer helping me heal. it is preventing it. it is the anchor that is pulling me to the bottom of the lake. writing about you is not stitching wounds anymore, it is ripping those same wounds open again. and i cannot keep allowing that to happen.

i've come to accept that i'm doing more damage to myself than you are, now. i'm becoming my own ghost. i am resurrecting you for no reason other than the fact that i think it may give me some good poems. and of course it does. it always does. but art is no longer an excuse to traumatize myself. it just can't be.

you are going to be there for the rest of my life. i will always be afraid of seeing you around every corner. and there will be times that i will. i have to live with it. i have to. those moments when we see each other will be some of the scariest moments of my life, and no amount of poetry can stop that from being the case. you will always be one of my greatest fears.

i don't think, hundreds of poems later, that i understand any better what makes you hurt people the way you do. i don't understand why i let you destroy me any more than i did when you were ripping me to shreds. i can write a hundred more and it will never make the slightest bit of sense to me.

i think this might just be a goodbye. a part of me will always love you. a part of me will always hate you. and those two halves will go to war every single morning when i wake up, and in every single encounter with you i might have, for the rest of my fucking life. and that's okay. i hate it, but it's okay.

i don't know if i can wish you happiness just yet. i think, i think i wish you justice, first. i wish for your heart to be absolutely destroyed. i wish for all the pain you caused me, and her, and her, and her, and her, and her, and her, to come back on you all at once. and then, once you understand why i just can't *shut the fuck up about what we had*, why i've written a whole book and half of another one centered on the destruction you caused, then you can be happy. you can find a girl and marry her and grow old with her and do all the things you promised to do with me (and all of the others).

but when that break happens, i will know. we will all know. we will feel the ripple from wherever we are.

because all the love you took from us?

it will finally come back.

5

golden yellow

for the calm after the storm,
the sun breaking through the clouds—
a love meant to save,
but never meant to stay.

you found me when i was

b r

o

ke   n

ap a

r t

and held out your hand.

"come with me,"
you said,
"i will help put you back t   o g e t her."

you were the sun
after the storm,
blasting away the clouds
of gray
to fill me
with light.

but:
i don't believe in saviors—
the only person who can save me,
is me.

i started saving myself
when i realized i was trapped,
and began searching
for a way out.

you may have reached
your hand out to me,

but i saved myself
when i chose to take it.

—don't get it twisted

you were my reminder.

my reminder that
i deserve
good things
and good love.

my reminder that
there will always
be people who are
willing to give those
to me.

scene:

we are playing hide-and-seek—childish, i know. but it was a tradition to kick off the beginning of the summer. a strange thing perhaps, for upperclassmen in high school to be doing, but we don't care.

we find ourselves hiding together behind a bush, pressed up against the brick wall of a house.

you wrap your arms around me, and i can feel your heart pounding. "you're nervous," i say.

"of course i am," you respond, "i really like you."

"i really like you too." i smile up at you in the dying sunlight. "can i kiss you?"

"yes," you breathe, so we do, and i forget about the game and him and all the parts of me he broke, and i just feel you, for once, i feel something other than him when kissing somebody else, and that's when i know.

that's when i realize you would be the one to finally, finally set me free.

end scene

in you
i found
salvation

in you
i found
freedom

in you
i found
myself again
after being lost
for so
long

— our own version of hide-and-seek

i had forgotten how it felt:
to not be so afraid all the time.

afraid of being lied to,
of being manipulated,
of being left,
of not being enough.

but with you,
i didn't feel any of that fear.

i knew you were mine
from the second we kissed.

relationship status: it's getting better

i haven't felt this way in so long: happy with you (myself).

it's like a breath of fresh air, waking up in the morning and smiling at what i see.

sure, we have days, but they're becoming less and less frequent.

even when i am with him, he does not pull me away from you. he would never tear us apart.

i have found someone who won't make me choose between him and you.

word of advice #5:

you don't always need
passion
drama
an insanely romantic story

to have a good relationship

sometimes
it's better to forego all that
so you can have
trust
kindness
stability

sure
you can find someone
who gives you both

but when you have
to pick

pick the one that won't
break your heart

i loved someone
like you, once.

i took him for granted.

so with you,
i enjoyed every moment.

rest assured,
i did not leave a second
too soon.

self-love sometimes
likes to play a game
of hide-and-seek with me;

i find the love
for myself
in the strangest
of places:

behind the corner
of my mirror,
under the lid
of my powder,
tucked away between bedsheets.

and sometimes,
it takes a little
longer to find—
minutes, days,
even weeks,

but i always
find it in the end.

i always
bring it out
of its hiding place.

i figured out
who i truly was
when we were together

do not think
i have forgotten
your part in that

— i am grateful

i don't know if i ever loved you
with everything in me,
because i think he had jumbled
my heart into a pile of broken
machinery,

but just know:
i loved you the best i could.

even when things weren't
exactly working,
i loved you.

you wanted me
to pursue my dreams,
until it became clear
that meant
leaving you
behind,

and i couldn't be
with someone
whose support
was conditional.

— i stop for no one

the truth is,
we just weren't meant
to be forever.

it's an unpleasant
and heavy truth to face,
and i know it hurt
to fold your hands around,
to understand it in its entirety.

that's the hardest part
about the end of your first love:

realizing that most of the time,
love is a time bomb.

it always hurts,
realizing that you're
temporary.

it doesn't get any easier
as the years go by.

even when you know
it's not going to last,
you see eternity in the people
you know you'll have to leave,
anyway.

— human nature

you don't have to be
a permanent fixture
in someone's life
to change them

those who
walk away
without blood
on their hands
are just as impactful
as the ones
who don't

sometimes
the most important loves
are the ones not meant
to stay

i tried my hardest to make sure
your first waltz with love
was as simple and delicate
as possible.

i kept us in time
with the music.

i showed you the right ways
to move, to touch, to sway.
the correct order of steps.

i did not step on your toes
(not too many times, at least).

there was no stumbling.
no falling.
no breaking
or hurting.

at the end of the song
i walked you to the edge
of the floor.
thanked you for dancing with me.
wished you happiness.
said your next dance partner
was a very lucky girl.

and then,
just like that,
i vanished into the crowd.

just like that,
i let you go.

as easily and painlessly
as i had come along.

you and i stood at a precipice.

i was entering a new chapter of my life, and you couldn't follow me. you know that now, right? there was suddenly an entire ocean between us, with no bridge to cover it. we were falling apart at the seams from straining at the distance.

i was leaving my childhood behind.
so i had to leave you.

i just had to.

things that remind me of you #5

sunlight / fresh air / genuine kindness / healing / nature /
people being nice to animals / learning love can be good again
/ being someone's first / understanding the importance of
everything you do / realizing your path /

/ relearning my worth /
/ relearning my skin /
/ relearning my heart /

/ ticking clocks /
/ running out of time /
/ always running out of time /

/ walking away /
/ not looking back /
/ smiling as i shut the door behind me /

what made me change
for you?

what turned me
from a friend
into an enemy?

what transformed us
from a fond memory
into your worst nightmare?

i am not the perfect lover.

i am bossy, sometimes insensitive, often overbearing.

these are my flaws, and i carry them.

so with you, i was not the perfect lover.

but i was not what you have made me out to be.

i picked you up when you were down.
i reminded you of the good things you had when you felt like
there was nothing there.
i made sure you always had a place to go when your own home
felt like a prison cell.
i supported you through everything. even after the breakup.
you came to me for advice that you knew nobody else could
give.

i am not asking to be put on a pedestal for these things. i
treated you right. that's all. i was good to you.

i am just asking for proper remembrance.
for respect.

i never wanted you to be bitterly stuck on me.

i just want us to die like we lived—with kindness and
understanding, always.

i do not deserve
this bullshit.

i do not deserve
to be remembered
like this.

—and you fucking know it

we were golden yellow
until you threw black paint
all over the canvas

—you ruined it

first loves
don't have to
be traumatic
or heartbreaking.

first loves
don't have to
leave you reeling
and scrambling
to put yourself
back together again.

they can be easy.
they can be set down
with grace.

—the pain isn't mandatory

i understand heartbreak. i have looked it right in its face as it has ripped its claws into me and left me shredded. i am well-acquainted with the pain that comes after. i know how it feels to have a first love die. i have felt its heart stop beating in my own hands. i have buried many more in the ground. and i treat the few that ended kindly very delicately. i know how rare it is to be able to walk away without anything more than a scratch. so i understand heartbreak. and i know that sometimes you hurt people more than you might think, and i know that sometimes the pain doesn't come until later, until much later.

but dammit, we were fine. we were fine until suddenly you decided we weren't, and i understand heartbreak, and trauma, and i even understand needing space, but we were fine. you can need space but still know that we were fine. you don't have to rewrite our story as ugly and broken to not want to be around me anymore. you can say we shouldn't be friends without telling everyone i'm a horrible person. sometimes needing space doesn't need an explanation other than the fact that you need it.

i understand heartbreak. i have watched it gut me and leave me for dead. i have sat awaiting its arrival time and time again. so when i thought i might have hurt you more than i thought, when i thought i might have been cruel to you in the slightest, i walked through all of us, from start to finish. and even at my worst, on my ugliest of days, i was kind to you. and never, never did i fail.

i have had a first love die in my hands. i have been held in a chokehold by pain.

and dammit, we were fine.

we were just fine.

i hope
one day

i rest easy
with you

— as i always intended

to golden yellow,

before i was your first love, i was your friend. and at the core
of our relationship, we were friends. the best of. i cherished
our friendship so much, that i made an effort to keep it alive
after we broke up. i had never done that before. before, when
a relationship ended, i walked away entirely. i ignored the fact
that i was losing a friend as well as a love. i believed that after
some point, one could not exist without the other. but with
you . . . i wanted to strip the love part of us away, eventually. i
wanted to keep the friendship. i wanted to keep *you*.

i know i seemed distant, but i was doing it to protect you. i
know it seemed like i pushed you away, but i knew you wouldn't
be able to move on if i didn't give you the space to. and i think,
in your heart, you understood that. i don't know if you wanted
to, though. and i get why. it seemed as if i was playing a cruel
game with you, but i wasn't. i promise i wasn't.

i don't know when you decided you had to hate me to be able to
let go. i don't know who told you that was a good idea. because
let me tell you something: the lovers i have tried to hate are the
ones that have stuck to me the longest. i think that is the case
with most people.

so if you never want to talk to me again, then that's okay. i won't
hate you back. i couldn't. i owe you nearly everything, and that
doesn't change—not now, not ever. but i won't miss you. i won't
beg forgiveness for a crime i didn't commit. i won't dwell.

i walked away three summers ago because i knew our love was
over. i have become good at recognizing the writing on the wall
when it comes to that type of thing. i guess i am not as good at
recognizing the writing when it comes to friendships.

maybe one day you'll realize it's a lot easier to hate people who actually did something to deserve it, and a lot harder to smear hatred on the faces of those you're just trying to stop loving.

6

emerald green

for the planting of a sapling

of a love that was going to

take root and grow,

and last and last and last.

the one before you helped shine sunlight on my leaves.

but you are the one who made me blossom.

—everlasting

one of the first nights
i told you
about the ones
who came before

i told you
about the first
how he gave me
my first taste
of love
only to take it away
so cruelly

i told you
about the second
how he taught me
that love takes
work
patience
and time

i told you
about the third
how he showed me
that love could
be calm and simple
and let down easily

i told you
about the fourth
how he destroyed me
and gave me wounds
that have yet
to finish
healing

i told you
about the fifth
how he showed me
that love could save
and give you hope
when you thought
you'd lost it

you asked
what do you think
i will show you

i told you
i think you will show me
that love
can last

listen to me:

it is okay
to take time
for yourself

to look deep
into the roots
of your soul

to examine
the vines stretching
out under your skin

to pick out
the weeds sprouting
in your mind

there is nothing
selfish about
tending to
your own garden

it is okay to
take the time
you need
to grow

scene:

it's a few nights before i release my first book. we are lying in my bed and i am reading it to you. every poem.

and you never once look away from me. you never once act bored or disinterested. you listen to every word, tell me what you think of each piece. sometimes, you stop me, ask me who the poem is about. who they are. who they were.

and i tell you. we've only been together for about a month, but i tell you everything.

you are not afraid of anything i say. not afraid, or jealous, or upset.

you say, "that poem was beautiful."

you say, "it's an honor to have you write about me."

you are the only one who's ever said that to me.

you are the only one to not shy away from what i have to say.

end scene

it's been over two years
since our first kiss
but i still remember
every moment:

your eyes, before.
my heart, during.
our love, after.

our love, still.

find someone
who breathes fire
into you,

who leaves embers simmering
in your rib cage,

who traces sparks
down your spine.

find someone who matches
your flame with one
just as powerful.

if you asked me to,
i would rip stars out of the sky
and slip them into your pockets.

if you needed it,
i would pull the salt from the ocean.
pour it into a shaker just for you.

i would give you the planets
on a silver platter.

whatever you desire.

just ask.

the moment
you begin to
love yourself
is an act of war

against those who try
to chain you to a scale,

against those who try
to brand you with a label,

against those who try
to tell you it is better
to do the opposite.

call yourself beautiful.

let it be your battle cry.

i look at you
and i do not see
an end.

only us,
beginning
and beginning
again.

—this is forever

i think
if you left me
i wouldn't feel
a thing.

not because
i wouldn't care.

but because
you might just take
too much of me
with you.

— *without you i am incomplete*

do you think time stops for us? do you think it understands the importance of moments and it slows to let us cherish them just a little bit longer? do you think that's why it felt like an eternity when we touched? i wonder if time saw you in my future and slammed on the brakes. i think maybe this time, time decided to stop at the red light instead of barreling right through like it usually does. maybe time decided, "maybe i want to see this." maybe time leaned back to enjoy the show.

it's incredible,
the amount of growing
you can do
when you're with
somebody who isn't
afraid of what you'll
become once you
bloom.

i have this theory about atoms and soul mates.

i think when you're drawn to somebody, it's because at one time, your atoms made up the same thing, be it a tree, or a dinosaur, or another person—your atoms and their atoms were interwoven together.

so as matter is reformed and recreated throughout time, your atoms are continuously pulled towards their atoms. sometimes they come together to form another flower or animal, and sometimes they bring two people together like magnets.

there's a pull between us that i don't think can be explained otherwise.

something about us is so purely scientific, so perfectly chemical.

the bond between us could be a chemist's wet dream.

word of advice #6:

the right love
can take its time
to arrive
to take root
and grow

you will
dig up
so many
loves that looked
pretty from afar
but once
you got closer
you saw
that they were rotting
from the inside out

but one day
you will find
the right love
for you

one day
what looks beautiful
from far away
will be just as beautiful
when it is held
in your own
two hands

when you find
someone who
does not make you
so afraid of the future

try your hardest
to not let
them go

i find hope
in the smallest of things:

in cracked sidewalks
and parted branches.

the bubbles in latte foam
and the lace of a dress.

i search for it
in between the cracks
and the pits
and the breaks,
always.

that is where
it is often hiding,
not usually found.

i am obsessed with the marks i leave on people,
just as i am obsessed with the marks people leave on me.

this has never made much sense to you, i know.
you don't understand why i care what he thinks of me,
but it's my mark. whatever he is saying, that is my mark,
and i care about what that looks like.

i am a writer and i once wrote that i cling.
i cling to bad memories like old stuffed animals
but i am still very much here with you.
i write about heartbreaks that haven't hurt me in years
as easily as i write about the one that still does,
and it is because i know how to cling.
they left their mark.

i am sentimental to a fault,
but do not think it is because i don't love you.
i look back on my past and admire it
because it has brought me to you.
i pay it tribute in my poems
because look who it has given me.
the love i feel every day.
to hold someone without
being afraid they'll slip away.

your mark.

— marks

things that remind me of you #6

rose quartz / tinder miracles / a lock hanging on a bridge in
salzburg / the feeling of knowing somebody better than you
know yourself / local coffee shops / sleepless nights / unfailing
devotion to your art / having a plan / trying new things /

/ a love that is both passionate and simple /
/ a love that is both burning and soft /
/ a love that is both exhilarating and calm /

/ being loud in your love /
/ not swallowing anything down anymore /
/ the future /

/ the future /
/ the future /

my mother is always wary of who i date because she wants
them to be able to match me. i have always been a lot to handle,
like a forest fire. you cannot put me out. boys have tried, not
because they want to tear me down but because i am all flash
and bang and large, sucking life out of rooms with my loud
mouth—big mouth, *god do you ever stop talking?* and the
answer is no, i don't, because i have a lot to say and not a lot
of time. i say i don't have a lot of time because i am a natural
disaster, or a man-made one, depending on how you look at it.
i am a tsunami, with waves and flooding and swamp. i stand
over people and they run—arrogance, *you're acting out of
place.* bitch, i am not, unkind royals never last that long; ever
read a history book? i will rip you out of your throne like it's
my fucking job. don't get comfortable up there; i'm swimming
around you like a shark. my teeth are sharp and i am ready
to taste blood. i am a plane that is probably crash landing,
all bump and jerk and fall, unpredictable and scary—is it
turbulence or am i actually falling apart. who knows, we'll find
out soon i guess. so my mom wants me to find a guy to match
me, because i tend to crush them beneath my thumb and not
even know it. i rip their spines out and use them as toothpicks
and then complain that they won't stand up to me, because
i haven't realized i have taken away their ability to stand. my
friends would defend them, say they're blind with love, and
i would laugh and say, *no, i don't want somebody who can't
see me, i want somebody who loves me but still does.* i have a
colossal amount of problems and messes, hence the numerous
comparisons to disasters, and i want somebody who can look
me in the eye and say, *whoa there cowboy, you're getting a
little out of hand,* rather than smile and tell me i'm beautiful
when i am clearly not acting beautiful. like, bitch, i know i'm
beautiful, i don't need you to tell me that, i need you to tell me
i'm being mean to you, i need you to tell me i'm not being the

best person, i need you to stop letting me swallow houses whole before you even get through the door. so anyway, i found this guy on tinder and it turns out he's really good at that. he's the firefighters to my fire, but like, firefighters who aren't super good at their job so they just quell the fire rather than put it out. he's the copilot to my probable plane crash, and he always steers me out of it. i think i've found my match. when i open my mouth and start to swallow, he pinches my lips closed and says, *hey, i love you but leave some for the rest of us.*

— an ode to being a lot to handle and finally finding the person who can handle it

i refuse
to be scared
of my own
reflection.

my body is not
something to
hide.

never again
will i find
myself

ugly
gross
too little
too much.

i will never
see myself
as anything less
than

beautiful.

—finally

i find
something sacred
in every second
we share

it keeps this love
ethereal

your match
is out there
somewhere

it may just be waiting
to be ignited

—the first spark

people always say:

you can't love somebody
until you love yourself

and this is wrong.

i've loved many
when i could hardly
look at myself in the mirror.

but when you love yourself,
loving another is easy,
like getting new glasses.

you can see the treetops
so much clearer.

it's so much easier
to read the fine print,
to understand the small moments.

it becomes so much easier
to recognize a truly good thing,

and a wolf in sheep's clothing.

i put a lock on a bridge
in salzburg austria
with our names
scribbled on it
in permanent ink

i put a lock on a bridge
in a city i dream of
every day
a city i may not
get to see again
for years

i put a lock on a bridge
in a city
that felt more like home
than my birthplace

i wrote the name of the boy
who stole my heart
on a lock on a bridge
in the city
that stole my entire being

does that not
tell you
how much
i believe in us

you call me beautiful
not because you think
i need to hear it
not because you think
i don't believe it

you call me beautiful
because you want me to know
you agree

—i am beautiful

you are the one thing
i want to just make it.

i could live without you,
but god,
i really don't want
to have to.

to the city
that reignited my love
for life
and music
and people:

i dream of you
when i sleep
and i wish for you
every morning
and every evening

i walk the streets here
and wish that they pulsed
with music as yours do

i look out my window
and yearn for the alps
and the blue of the salzach

i want to go home
i want to go home
i want to go home

and i swear to god
one day
i am going
to come back
to you

— ode to salzburg

this year, i hang my mirror directly across from my bed. when i lie amongst the blankets, i can watch myself. i am the first thing i see when i wake up every morning. there is a comfort in that, something that makes me feel real.

sometimes, i stare at my reflection while i am naked. stripped down to skin, everything soft and smooth. i trace my fingers over the dimples in my thighs and fat across my stomach. my hands will dance over my chest, and i think there is something special in touching your own body—you will never know somebody else's more than you know your own. i find that both beautiful and terrifying. i hate to think of all the treasure i gifted those who had me when i did not know my own worth, how many times i left it up to somebody else to figure my body out because i did not find myself wanting to give it the time it deserved.

i think, now, i am redeeming myself.

relationship status: taken and happy.

we made it.

i know that it was hard. i know i was not always that kind to you (myself). but thank you for sticking around. thank you for staying while i tried to find my way back to you.

i see you and i see the rest of my life, now. there is no doubt.

i know now that you are the only one who will be here, always.

i know now that that is nothing to be afraid of.

i love you. i'm sorry. thank you.

i love you (me).

to emerald green,

i don't feel the need to write a particularly long letter. the others have been goodbyes, but we have no need for that. we never will.

there is so much to say that i will never be able to really articulate. you do that to me, always have. there's so many things i want to tell you that i cannot say with others listening.

i don't think we make sense to some people. you are messy where i am clean, and i am caged where you are free. but we move like clockwork. i scrub away the dirt and you break open my locks. to anyone who bothers to look a little closer, we work better than anybody.

you have loved me in the perfect way. you allow me to grow, to stand tall, to bloom, but you keep me rooted. you keep me humble. but you never, ever tear me down. and that is how i always hope to love you.

i love you, always.

thank you for letting me become the person i was always meant to be.